CHARLES DICKENS'
A CHRISTMAS CAROL
IN EASY READING VERSE

By the same author:

Shakespeare's Tragedies in Easy Reading Verse

Shakespeare's Comedies in Easy Reading Verse

Shakespeare's Histories & Romances in Easy Reading Verse

Shakespeare's Sonnets in Easy Reading Verse

Chaucer's Canterbury Tales in Easy Reading Verse

Charles Dickens' Oliver Twist in Easy Reading Verse

Kenneth Grahame's The Wind in the Willows in Easy Reading Verse

CHARLES DICKENS'
A CHRISTMAS CAROL
in Easy Reading Verse

Richard Cuddington

Cover design by Denis Grigorjuk
Title page illustration by Michael Avery

Published by CompletelyNovel.com

ISBN 9781849149587

Contents

MARLEY WAS DEAD FOR SURE!

So let us start by saying,
Marley was dead for sure.
Expired, deceased, completely dead,
Not living any more.

For at his solemn funeral,
Why even Scrooge had kneeled –
And notice of the burial,
It had been signed and sealed…

And by the Clerk – the Clergyman –
The Undertaker too,
And even Scrooge, that dismal wretch
Had signed as was his due.

So nothing now could contradict –
In any way assail –
The bare, cold fact that Marley was
Dead as an old door-nail!

Yes, Marley had departed life,
He'd gone behind death's veil,
And this must be completely known
To understand this tale.

For nothing wonderful can come
From all I am to tell,
Unless you take on board the fact
That Marley was in hell…

Or maybe even heaven,
It makes no difference for –
The only thing you need to know –
Marley was dead for sure!

EBENEZER SCROOGE

Years passed by and still it stayed,
The sign upon the door:
Scrooge and Marley – there it was,
Though Marley lived no more.

For Scrooge was much too tight to pay
To have the sign amended,
So Scrooge's name stayed on the sign
With *Marley* still appended.

And what of Scrooge, what can we say?
What kind of man was he?
We'll need to choose words carefully,
So now then – let me see.

Well he was wrenching, grasping,
Covetous – clutching too,
And squeezing, scraping, miserly,
A sinner through and through.

Hard eyed and sharp as any flint,
Secret and self contained –
With solitary bearing and
A face all stern and strained.

A soul within like freezing ice –
So cold inside it froze
His features into shrivelled cheeks
And nipped his pointed nose.

It made his eyes all red and raw,
His mean, thin lips turn blue,
And when he spoke in rasping voice
It chilled all those he knew.

And when he walked with stiffened gait
He drew along with him,
A cold, low temperature that clung
Like something rank and grim.

No wind that blew was bitterer,
No snow fell colder than
The awful chilling atmosphere
That clung to this dire man.

Nobody stopped him in the street,
And said, 'How do you do?
How goes the world with you dear Scrooge –
My dear chap – how are you?'

No beggar asked him for some coins.
No children asked the time.
It was as though they thought he might
Be guilty of a crime.

The dogs of blind men even,
(Which are a special breed)
Would lead their owners far away
By tugging on their lead.

Did any of this worry Scrooge?
Did he think it unfair?
Well no – it didn't bother him –
He really didn't care.

SCROOGE RECEIVES AN INVITATION

It was that special time of year
When all good folk perceive,
A season of great merriment –
For it was Christmas Eve.

Grim Scrooge sat in his Counting House
All bent and thin and old.
Outside was foggy – biting wind –
So bleak and very cold.

He heard the people stamping
Out in the freezing street,
Trying anything they could
To raise a little heat.

And though it was but three o'clock
The sky was growing dark,
And fog was lying soupy thick;
The world looked very stark.

The door of Scrooge's counting room
Was open just a bit
So he could see the chair on which
His lowly clerk did sit.

This poor, sad soul just shivered there
As he worked every day,
For he had but a little fire
To keep the cold at bay.

Scrooge wouldn't pay to keep him warm,
So all the clerk could do
Was hover near his candle and
Hope it might warm him through.

A vain and useless hope for sure,
But that's just how things were
If you were so unfortunate
To work for such a cur.

But then in one swift movement
The front door opened wide;
A young man stood there shivering,
Then quickly stepped inside.

'A Merry Christmas uncle,'
Old Scrooge's nephew said.
'Bah, humbug,' Scrooge replied as he
Bad tempered, shook his head.

'Christmas a humbug uncle?'
The nephew then replied.
'I can't believe that's what you think.
In fact, I think you lied.'

'Of course I mean it,' Scrooge cried out.
'A Merry Christmas – puff!
How can you say you're merry
When you are poor enough?'

'But why should you be so morose?'
The nephew cried with glee.
'For you are rich enough and thus
You should agree with me.

'So don't be angry uncle.'
Old Scrooge replied with ire,
'I'll keep Christmas how I like –
You do as you desire.

'As far as I'm concerned all those
With Christmas on their lips,
Should boil in their own pudding,
In the pot – up to their hips.

'I'll keep Christmas how I like,
Just leave me here alone.'
'You don't keep it,' his nephew cried.
'You spend it on your own.'

'And that's just fine,' old Scrooge replied.
'For that's just what I'll do.
And you can please yourself – although
Much good will it do you.'

'Dear uncle,' said the nephew,
'Please don't make such a fuss,
Why don't you come tomorrow and
Spend Christmas Day with us?'

The clerk on hearing this clapped hands.
Scrooge stared at him right through.
'You'll lose your job if I should hear
Another peep from you.'

Then turning to his nephew
Scrooge said in nasty tone,
'I wouldn't come for anything,
I'd rather be alone.

'I bid you sir, good afternoon.
Our dialogue now ends!'
His nephew said, 'But uncle, please,
Why can't we just be friends?'

'I said good afternoon,' Scrooge rasped.
His manner reeked of gloom.
'A Happy New Year,' came reply –
The nephew crossed the room.

And on his way he stopped to say
A kindly word unto
The poor, downtrodden clerk – he said,
'Glad tidings sir, to you.'

Though he was cold and shivering
The clerk gave warm reply,
For some are cordial in distress
And who can fathom why?

As Scrooge's nephew left, he let
Two portly fellows in.
Each had a pleasant countenance
With red and ruddy skin.

'*Scrooge and Marley's* I believe,'
One of the fellows said.
'Yes it is,' old Scrooge replied,
'But Marley sir, is dead.

'He died some seven years ago
Upon this very night.'
He shook his head impatiently
And his pursed lips turned white.

'Well I'm sure his living partner,'
The other man replied,
'Will prove to be as generous
As he who's sadly died.

'We're raising money for the poor.
'Tis proper thing to do.
So tell me sir, what sum should I
Be putting down for you?'

'Nothing!' came the curt reply
From Scrooge – and hastily.
'I don't support such charities
So you'll get naught from me.

'I do not celebrate this time
Or give my cash away;
Idle folk must sort themselves,
So leave me be, I say.

'There's room within the Workhouse
As you and I both know;
There's shelter offered there – that's where
These idle folk should go.'

'Many would much rather die.'
One of the fine men said.
Scrooge made a noise and then exclaimed,
'They'd all be better dead.

'If they would rather die, they'd best
Do it right away –
Decrease the population –
That sirs, is what I say.'

The gentlemen were quite amazed
And wondered what to do,
But seeing Scrooge's scowling face
They tactfully withdrew.

The afternoon dragged slowly on –
Scrooge sat there looking sour –
Until the chiming of the clock
Informed it was the hour…

To end the working day, it had
Now reached the time to close.
He looked at his downtrodden clerk
And said, 'Well, I suppose…

You want to take tomorrow off.'
He said this to infer
That it was quite unreasonable;
The clerk replied, 'Yes sir.

'If that would be convenient.'
'It's not,' old Scrooge replied.
'But no more than expected.'
The clerk just meekly sighed.

'If I stopped you a half a crown,'
Scrooge then went on to say,
'You'd think that I was being unfair.
You'd still demand your pay.

'And yet you don't think I'm ill used
When I give you your wage
And get no work back in return.
It is a gross outrage.'

The clerk replied most quietly
And with a little fear,
'Christmas is a special time
And comes but once a year.'

Said Scrooge, 'That is a poor excuse,
But I give you fair warning,
If you must have the whole day off
Come earlier next morning.'

The clerk replied he would and Scrooge
Walked out and with a growl,
Giving cash away had turned
His mood from bad to foul.

The office door was locked and then
Scrooge strode off with a frown,
While his poor clerk set out for home
Which was in Camden Town.

MARLEY'S GHOST

Scrooge had a sorry dinner in
A tavern quite close by;
A dreary, melancholy place –
Just like a dank pigsty.

And then he headed homeward to
His suite of gloomy rooms.
They had the feel of something dire,
Like dark and awful tombs.

He walked into the dismal yard,
Towards his large front door;
The fog still swirled – the yard was dark,
He shivered to his core.

Upon the door a knocker shone,
As large as any seen,
But as Scrooge turned his key he saw
Where knocker once had been…

A face! A face? 'Twas Marley's face!
As clear as any day,
And he was staring out, though not
In a ferocious way.

But it was scary all the same,
It had a horrid look,
As Scrooge stood there and stared right back
His whole thin body shook.

He wondered for a moment then
Had he gone quite insane?
He rubbed his eyes and looked away
And then he looked again.

And now the face had disappeared.
It was no longer there.
The vision on the door had gone
And vanished into air.

To say Scrooge wasn't startled
Would not be true at all;
He was and quickly pushed the door
And stepped into his hall.

When nothing awful lurked behind
The heavy, wooden door,
He muttered, 'Pah!' – his manner changed
To how it was before.

He closed the door behind him,
Then made his careful way
Up the massive staircase which –
It would be true to say…

Was wide enough to drive a coach
With horses there as well,
Right up between the banisters
And going at pell-mell.

Scrooge trimmed his little candle
For all was grey and stark;
(It saved him money if he kept
His rooms ill lit and dark).

He made his way around the house
To see that all was right,
And thankfully he found no-one
Was lurking there that night.

Once satisfied he closed the door
And locked it from within,
Then pulled on his old dressing gown
And yanked it to his chin…

For it was cold – the fire contained
Hardly any fuel,
So he sat very close to eat
His meagre plate of gruel.

As he ate he looked above
To where there hung a bell;
It had been placed there long ago
And why he couldn't tell.

His eye was drawn – and slowly then,
The bell began to swing.
At first the long forgotten bell
Just swung – it didn't ring.

But soon it rang out loud and clear,
Then it was joined as well
By others ringing through the house –
By every other bell.

The noise reverberated through
Each locked and padlocked door.
It seemed to last an hour but was
A minute – nothing more.

Once they had ceased Scrooge thought perhaps
They would start up again,
But then he heard another noise –
The clanking of a chain.

It sounded like it dragged along
The stone flagged cellar floor.
Scrooge thought he'd heard that ghosts were forced
To drag chains as a chore.

And then he heard the cellar door
Fly open with a boom,
And then the noise was coming from
The floor beneath his room.

And then the dragging sound was heard
Coming up the stairs;
Scrooge thought he'd build a barricade
Against the door with chairs.

But then he cried, 'It's humbug.'
And then with dropping jaw
He saw an apparition
Pass slowly through the door.

He stared for in his mind great doubt
And scorn were uppermost.
He seemed to hear the fire cry out,
'See there – it's Marley's Ghost.'

And yes, it was the very same,
Marley, for sure, although
He was a little different from
The man Scrooge used to know.

Yes true, his pigtail was still tied –
His clothes were as before,
But round his waist a chain hung down,
And then surprised Scrooge saw…

That Marley was transparent,
For he could look clear through;
But still old Scrooge denied the sight,
Convinced it wasn't true.

'How now!' cried Scrooge – caustic and cold,
'What do you want with me?'
'Much!' 'Twas Marley's voice for sure –
But in an eerie key.

'Who are you?' Scrooge asked nervously.
'Ask who I *was*,' it said.
'Who were you then?' Scrooge raised his voice,
'When alive – not dead!'

'Well, I was Jacob Marley,
Your partner,' Marley sighed.
'And was for many countless years
Until that day I died.

'I see you don't believe me.'
'I don't,' replied old Scrooge.
'This is a mere delusion,
A mirage! – Subterfuge.'

At this the spirit raised a cry,
It chilled Scrooge to the bone,
For it was an appalling noise,
Half wailing – half a groan.

And then the ghost in one swift move
Undid a bandage that
Was tied around his head – his jaw
Dropped on his chest – whereat…

Scrooge fell upon his knees and clasped
His hands before his face.
He grovelled on the floor afront
The towering fireplace.

'Mercy! Mercy!' he cried out.
'Dreadful apparition,
Why trouble me? I beg of you
Pity my condition.'

'Do you believe in me or not?'
The ghastly spirit said.
'I do, I do,' Scrooge, trembling, cried.
His voice now reeked of dread.

'But why do spirits walk the earth?
Why do you come to me?'
'It is required of everyone,'
The ghost said quietly.

'To do a penance at some time,'
His eerie voice then soared,
'To let the spirit deep within
Take time to walk abroad…

'And go amongst his fellow men,
And travel far and wide,
And let his better sentiments
Direct and be his guide.

'For if a man does not go forth
While he has life and breath,
He is condemned to roam the world
Following his death.

'A woeful thing – for he must then
See things he cannot share.'
The spectre clanked his heavy chain
And cried out in despair.

Scrooge shook with fear but had to ask,
'You're fettered. Tell me then,
Why do you drag that heavy chain?
Does that await all men?'

'I wear the chain I forged in life,
And every doleful clink
Reminds me that I made it all,
Each yard – and link by link.

'For every loop here represents
The mean, cold life I led,
Filled up with selfishness and greed,'
The ghost, with sorrow, said.

Scrooge trembling, just cowered there;
The ghost went on to say,
'Your chain grows longer all the time,
Increasing every day.

'For seven Christmas Eve's ago
You'd managed to obtain
A length and heaviness like mine –
A truly ponderous chain.

'Since then you've laboured every day,
And every day it's grown,
Until you now possess a chain
So long – it stands alone.'

Scrooge looked around as if to search
For links upon the floor,
But saw just mangy carpet there
And floorboards – nothing more.

'Jacob, speak to me,' he cried.
'Oh Jacob Marley please,
Speak comfort to this wretched soul.
Bring my poor mind some ease.'

'I have no ease to offer you.
No comfort for your soul.
You'll need the help of other ghosts
To thus achieve this goal.

'I can now offer little more.
I cannot rest or stay.
I cannot linger anywhere
So I must be away…

'For in my life I never left
Our money-changing hole;
Now weary journeys lie ahead
If I'm to save my soul.

'A captive, bound and double-ironed –
If only I had known,
I would have lived a better life
But now that chance has flown.

'And so I travel onwards
Upon my endless course;
No rest, no peace and tortured by
The anguish of remorse.'

'You were a businessman,' Scrooge cried,
'And one who didn't shirk,
So why should you be suffering
For doing honest work?'

'Business! Business!' cried the ghost.
'In life I was so blind,
For if aware I would have seen
My business was Mankind.

'Why did I walk amidst great crowds
With taut and selfish frown,
With no thought for my fellow man
And with my eyes turned down?'

Scrooge was very much dismayed
To hear the spectre's plea,
But then it cried, 'My time is short
So Scrooge – attend to me.

'For I have come along tonight
Before it is too late
To warn you how to find a way
To thus escape my fate.'

'Oh thank'ee, thank'ee,' Scrooge replied.
'I would not share your end,
 I count on you to guide me as
 A true and honest friend.'

The ghost continued then and said,
'You will be haunted by
Three ghosts – who soon will visit you.'
Old Scrooge then asked him 'Why?'

'They have to come for if they don't,'
Translucent Marley said,
'You do not have the slightest chance
To shun the path I tread.

'Expect the first tomorrow,
When one o'clock doth strike.'
Scrooge said, 'It doesn't seem to be
A visit I will like.

'Can't I take them all at once –
Just see them in one go?'
The ghost was quite emphatic for
Its answer flew back 'No!

'The second spirit will then come
Upon the second night,
And then the third will too appear
And come within your sight.

'This will be upon the stroke
Of twelve – and it will be
The next night from the second ghost
Thus making up the three.

'So look to see me no more for
My task is now complete.
I do not think that e'er again
The two of us will meet.'

Then Marley took the bandage
And tied it round his jaw,
Then gathered up his chain and made
The clanking sound once more;

And then he tottered backwards
And as he did Scrooge saw
The window open slowly and –
He heard a great uproar.

The ghost waved Scrooge to now draw near
And when their two pale faces
Were very close – in fact as close
As just within two paces…

He raised his arm; Scrooge stopped right there,
Then in surprise and fear,
He heard the noises once again
And they were drawing near.

He heard such incoherent sounds
All floating in the air,
Lamentations – cries of woe,
Wailing everywhere.

Jacob Marley listened then
To the dire, mournful dirge.
All the cries and awful moans
Now seemed to join and merge.

And then he wailed – then floated out
Into the bleak dark night,
And very quickly disappeared
From frightened Scrooge's sight.

But though he was afraid and though
Old Scrooge still gasped and shook,
He couldn't stop himself at all
From taking just a look.

And when he did, with great surprise
He saw that everywhere,
Were phantoms floating aimlessly
Out on the cold night air.

They wandered thus, accompanied by
The woeful, doleful strains
Of their wails and each one had
A belt of heavy chains…

Just like the one that Marley wore;
They drifted miserably,
And as they did old Scrooge could tell
That none of them were free.

For each was captive to his past
With its remembered pain,
And captive too and held in check
By its respective chain.

Scrooge recognised a few of them –
And one old ghost did chafe
Against the chain around his leg
Tied to a massive safe.

The ghost cried out most piteously
For in a doorway there
He'd seen a woman with a child
Who was in need of care.

He knew he couldn't give her aid.
This couldn't happen – never.
To help in human matters now,
He'd lost the power forever.

And then the spirits faded.
The wailing died as well,
And on the darkened city street
An eerie silence fell.

The street now just appeared to be
A calm and normal sight,
It looked just like it always did
When he walked home each night.

Scrooge closed the window hurriedly –
And then he checked the door
To see if it was still quite locked.
'Twas as it was before.

Double locked as he supposed.
The bolts were undisturbed.
He went to utter 'Humbug'
But this he quickly curbed.

He stopped at the first syllable,
Then made his way to bed –
With thoughts of ghosts and spirits
Now spinning through his head.

The night's events had tired him out.
He thought, 'All this can keep
Until tomorrow morning' – so,
He soon fell fast asleep.

THE FIRST OF THE THREE SPIRITS

When Scrooge woke up it was so dark
He couldn't see a thing,
And then he heard the church bell chime
With its distinctive ring.

The clanging notes gave sleepy Scrooge
A most surprising shock,
For they rang out the hour and chimed
That it was twelve o'clock.

'Why this is nigh impossible,'
Cried Scrooge – in quite a stew.
'For when I went to bed it was
Already well past two.

'I can't have slept throughout a day
Into another night,
But surely if that's not the case
The church bell can't be right.'

He scrambled from his bed and then
Groped his way to see
What was happening in the street;
He cried, 'It baffles me…

'For everything is peaceful here,
It seems there is no way
That night has beaten off somehow
The brightness of the day.'

Scrooge went back to bed again
And thought and thought just what
Was this about – was Marley's ghost
A dream or was it not?

Then as he lay there silently,
Nervous and undone,
He recalled the ghost had said
Some *thing* would come at one.

And so he lay there waiting
Until he heard 'Ding-dong',
'A quarter past,' Scrooge counted out,
'If I'm not far from wrong.'

And then he dozed a little more,
Then once again 'Ding-dong'.
Scrooge told himself and nervously,
'I really must stay strong.'

And so he lay impatiently,
And then at last 'Ding-dong'.
He said, 'It's now a quarter to,
It won't be very long.'

And then again a great 'Ding-dong'.
'The hour itself,' Scrooge said.
A light flashed then a hand drew back
The curtains of the bed.

It frightened Scrooge – oh I should say.
He sat up with a start.
He was so shaken as he felt
His swiftly pounding heart.

And then he found himself to be
Close-up and face to face,
With an unearthly visitor,
As close as to the place…

Where dear reader, I am now,
For I should let you know
I'm standing there in spirit by
Your side – at your elbow!

The figure was most strange indeed,
A child – and yet again
More like an old man with long hair
That hung down in a mane.

The arms were long and muscular,
On show – for they were bare,
And Scrooge could see its feet were too,
As it stood shoeless there.

It wore a tunic of pure white,
And tied around the waist
There was a belt of lustrous sheen;
Exquisite – in good taste.

But quite the strangest thing of all
To this amazing sight,
Was from the crown of its fine head
There shone a ray of light.

And this bright beam made possible
For all then to be seen,
But as Scrooge looked the Spirit changed
In substance and in sheen.

It sparkled, glowed and glittered
In one part then another,
It took one shape, then something else,
In one form then some other.

One moment it just seemed to have
One leg and one weird head,
Then it would change to three legs and
No head and arms instead.

And then it would in just a trice
Quite suddenly appear
As normal as a proper soul
And stand distinct and clear.

'Are you the Spirit?' Scrooge cried out,
'Of whom I was foretold?'
'I am,' the Spirit said – the voice
Was soft, not brusque or cold.

'I am the ghost of Christmas Past!'
'Long past?' came Scrooge's plea.
'No, no – *your* past,' came its reply,
'As soon, you'll come to see.'

'What business brings you here tonight?'
Scrooge grasped his old bedpost.
'Your welfare first and foremost,' said
This brightly shining ghost.

Scrooge thought, 'A night of peaceful rest
Was most of all my need.'
The ghost read Scrooge's mind, then said,
'First – reclamation – heed!'

It offered Scrooge a strong, firm hand
And also clasped his arm.
Scrooge felt great apprehension and
A feeling of alarm.

'Rise and walk with me,' it said.
Scrooge did as he was told.
It would have been a waste of time
To plead that it was cold.

So from his warm and cosy bed
He rose but lightly clad;
Just nightshirt, cap and dressing gown
Were all the clothes he had.

The spirit's grasp was gentle yet
It quietly insisted;
It would have made scant difference
If scared Scrooge had resisted.

Scrooge hung on firmly as they moved.
'For I might fall,' he said.
'Just hold on gently,' came reply,
'And follow where you're led.'

And so they floated upwards
And passed right through the wall,
And Scrooge no longer felt that he
Might take a fatal fall.

SCROOGE VISITS HIS OLD SCHOOL

When Scrooge then looked around he saw
They were in countryside;
The city had quite disappeared;
He cried out to his guide…

'Good heavens! I was bred right here –
Why in this very place.'
He clasped his hands, a tremor passed
Across his upturned face;

For he was quite enraptured
With all the hope and joy
That had been long forgotten,
Of when he was a boy.

With shaking voice Scrooge begged the ghost
'Just lead me where you may.'
The ghost replied impatiently,
'You recollect the way?'

'Remember it?' Scrooge cried – he felt
As if he had been scolded.
'I recall – why every inch,
For I could walk blindfolded.'

They walked along the road and Scrooge
Recalled each bush and tree,
And every gate and post – in fact
All that there was to see.

Then in the distance, through bare trees
With roots all gnarled and brown,
They saw what surely was a quaint
And ancient market town.

Scrooge's lip was trembling,
His body all a-quiver
As he glimpsed the little church
And bridge across the river.

He saw some boys on ponies –
They laughed as they passed by;
They called to friends in country gigs
Who answered with a cry.

Oh, what a merry scene it was
For every little boy,
Was filled with carefree happiness
And overpowering joy.

And music filled the air – in fact
That crisp and lovely air
Laughed to hear it – merriment
Was really everywhere.

The ghost said, 'These are shadows now
Of things that once have been;
They have no consciousness of us
And so we can't be seen.'

The joyful travellers rode on,
Scrooge knew them, every one,
And he rejoiced beyond all bounds
To see them having fun.

They cried, 'A Merry Christmas.'
And this time Scrooge was glad;
Perhaps in times of long ago
He hadn't been so bad.

The children passed on by – the ghost
Now seemed a mite concerted.
He said, 'Despite this happiness
Yon school is not deserted.

'A solitary child remains –
Left there against his will;
Neglected by his so called friends
For he remains there still.'

Scrooge cried, 'I know it to be true.'
He sobbed – the ghost then said,
'Let's go now to the school,' and Scrooge
Just followed where it led.

And when they reached the school they found
It was in disrepair;
Damp walls and broken windows,
Decay was everywhere.

On entering, they crossed the hall
And passed then through a door,
And right before them, there it was
That both of them now saw…

A long and melancholy room
With lines of desks and forms.
'Twas not the kind of place that tries
To welcome as it warms.

Oh no – for it was cold as ice
Despite a feeble fire;
It seemed that misery and damp
Had joined there to conspire…

To shape a scene of loneliness
In this unhappy hall,
Then place a hapless victim there,
Bereft – amongst it all.

For sitting on a wooden form,
Shivering and alone
A little boy was reading,
Quietly – on his own.

And Scrooge broke down and bleakly wept,
His mind was in a haze –
To see his long forgotten self
From those lost former days.

He let his tears fall freely,
His heavy heart was bleeding
To see his poor and tragic self
All alone there reading.

'I wish, oh how I wish,' he said
As he then looked around,
And dried his eyes upon his cuff
And made a sniffing sound;

'Oh yes, I wish but then again
It's too late now and so
I should just let it pass on by
And let the notion go.'

The Spirit said, 'So tell me Scrooge
What is the matter? – Why,
You seem completely out of sorts.'
Scrooge sighed a weary sigh.

'It's nothing really,' Scrooge replied,
'And yet this sorry sight
Reminded me about a boy
Who knocked my door last night.

'He stood there singing carols,
Alone and very small.
I wish I'd given him a gift –
Just something – that is all.'

The ghost smiled thoughtfully and said
As he then waved his hand,
'Let's see another Christmas now
To help you understand.'

And as Scrooge looked, the scene had changed,
His former self he saw,
In that same room but older now
And all alone once more;

But he no longer read, instead
He paced despairingly.
Rapt Scrooge looked at the ghost then back
To see what he would see.

And then the door burst open,
A little girl came in;
Blonde hair and very pretty
With soft and milky skin.

She threw her arms around his neck
And kissed him on the head.
'Dear brother, I have come today
To bring you home,' she said.

'Home, little Fan?' returned the boy.
'Yes,' said the child with glee.
'Father is much gentler now
So you can come with me.

'He spoke so kindly to me when
I went to bed one night,
So I was not afraid to ask
If he'd agree, you might…

'Come back to be at home once more
And live with us again,
And he said "Yes" and so I've come
To make it very plain…

'You do not have to suffer here –
Let Christmas be unfurled;
We'll be together and we'll have
The best time in the world.

'A coach is waiting outside now.'
She dragged him to the door.
'Get your trunk and everything,
You're finished here for sure.'

She clapped her hands in happiness
And as they left they said,
Goodbye to the schoolmaster,
Who bowed his sombre head.

The coach wheels spun and cut right through
The hoar-frost and the snow,
Oh such a happy Christmas scene
As off to home they go.

The ghost then said, 'She had a heart
So large and full of love,
And yet she was so delicate –
But truly way above…

'So many others in this world.'
'How right you are,' Scrooge cried.
The ghost went on, 'So sad indeed
The way the poor girl died.

'She was a woman, I believe,
But still so very young.
A mother though, despite her youth.'
Old Scrooge's head now hung.

'She had one child – aye just the one,'
Scrooge said with furrowed brow.
'It's true,' the ghost replied 'and he
Is your sole nephew now.'

Scrooge felt uneasy in his mind –
Quite troubled – nothing less.
He frowned in deep embarrassment
And tersely answered, 'Yes'.

FEZZIWIG'S JOYOUS CHRISTMAS

Although they'd only left the school
A moment just before,
They were now in a busy street –
And Christmas blazed once more.

For every shop was dressed and bright,
The air was cold and clear,
And everyone was bustling
With tidings of good cheer.

The ghost stopped at a warehouse door;
'You know it?' he then asked.
'Know it!' Scrooge cried out. 'Oh yes,
For herein I was tasked…

'With doing my apprenticeship –
A blessing on the place.'
They went inside and straightaway
Scrooge recognised a face.

'It's Fezziwig – oh bless his heart,
And he appears to thrive,
For once again he does appear
So very much alive.'

Old Fezziwig laid down his pen
And slowly he took stock.
He rubbed his hands and laughed out loud
And looked up at the clock.

It pointed to the hour of seven
Which caused him to rejoice.
He called out in a comfortable,
Rich, fat and oily voice.

'Yo ho there, Ebenezer!
And Dick!' His tone was light.
'Yo ho my boys – there'll be no more
A-working here tonight.'

Scrooge's former self came in –
A young man now – and he
Was with his fellow 'prentice
Who followed speedily.

'Dick Wilkins to be sure,' cried Scrooge.
'A faithful friend of mine.'
And then old Fezziwig called out
And raised a glass of wine.

'Let's have the shutters up now lads
For it is Christmas Eve.'
The two lads soon fulfilled the task
With an almighty heave.

'Clear everything away – make room,'
Old Fezziwig then cried.
'Pack all the desks and chairs away
And put them on the side.

'Stoke up the fire – trim all the lamps,
We'll make a ballroom here
Where we can celebrate with joy
This season of good cheer.'

A fiddler soon arrived and then
Mrs Fezziwig appeared,
With her three daughters beaming
To see the floor was cleared.

In came young men and women
As if it were by chance,
But all knew that this evening,
There'd be a Christmas dance.

In came the cook and milkman,
The housemaid came as well.
In strode the baker and the lad
Whose job it was to sell…

Chestnuts from a brazier –
And all were soon entranced,
As everyone chose partners,
Took to the floor and danced.

The room was filled with happiness –
With food and drink for all;
Wrapped in the joy of Christmas time –
As grand as any ball.

It lasted through the evening,
Oh such a happy sight,
A fun filled, warm and glowing
Quite magic, festive night.

And at the core of everything
Was Fezziwig – the man
Who spread the joy of Christmastide
As only good men can.

Then finally the clock chimed out –
The hour was now eleven,
So it was time to call a halt
To this small piece of heaven.

Mr and Mrs Fezziwig
Stood there by the door,
They both shook hands with all their guests
And wished them joy – and more.

They said 'A Merry Christmas.'
To every single one,
And everybody said they'd had
The most enormous fun.

Then finally the voices
So cheerful, died away.
Scrooge stood there hardly knowing
What in the world to say.

For as he'd watched he'd quickly been
Completely overcome;
Just mesmerised – entranced – beguiled
And almost struck quite dumb.

For he remembered everything –
Enjoyed it once again –
But he was agitated now
And felt regret and pain.

The ghost then spoke and archly said
With a dismissive ring,
'A trivial little party
Was such a silly thing.

'To think it made these simple folk
So full of gratitude.'
'What!' cried Scrooge – he didn't like
The ghost's light attitude.

'It's not a small thing – not at all.'
Old Scrooge was quick to say.
His manner was quite different from
His normal selfish way.

The ghost went on, 'All he has done
Is spend a pound or two.
Why should he earn such praise and from
Someone, the likes of you?'

'It's not like that,' Scrooge cried aloud.
Outrage was in his voice.
'For Fezziwig was able then
To make a different choice.

'He chose the path of happiness –
To spread it all around.
He made quite sure that merriment
Would flourish and abound.

'He had the power to make our toil
A pleasure or a chore.
To make it light or burdensome –
An awful menace or…

'A source of gentle harmony –
He chose to make life good.'
The spirit glanced at Scrooge and thought
Perhaps he understood.

SCROOGE'S SWEETHEART

And now they were outside again
Stood in a little court.
'We must be quick,' the ghost exclaimed,
'My time with you grows short.'

He said this more unto himself,
Then suddenly again –
Events moved on – the scene had changed
And Scrooge saw there, so plain…

His self of many years before,
A far off, former time.
He saw a figure – purposeful,
A man right in his prime.

His face was not as rigid
As later years – and yet
Already signs of avarice
Upon his face were set.

There was a restless motion
Deep in the young man's eyes;
Full of greed and menacing –
And his impatient sighs…

Showed the passion rooted there
And signalled most of all
The shadow of the growing tree
And how the tree would fall.

But he was not alone, he sat
With a girl, so fair,
Who gazed forlornly and then said,
'I know you do not care.

'Another has replaced me now
Which may bring comfort too,
As I had hoped to bring and would
Have tried my best to do.'

'Who has replaced you?' he enquired.
She shook as if with dread,
And looking at his frowning face,
'A golden one,' she said.

'You do not value normal gifts
Like love and joy and health;
Your life is given to one thing,
The rapt pursuit of wealth.

'We made a contract 'twixt ourselves
A long, long time ago,
When both of us were very poor,
But happy to be so.

'But now you've changed, you're not the man
I knew – you've lost the joy
That you had then.' He scowling said
'Why then I was a boy.'

'You know you're not the same,' she sighed,
'So sadly we must part,
For it is best this way although
It breaks my aching heart.

'And so I now release you, dear,
And hope you find true peace.'
He said, 'I do not understand –
For have I sought release?'

'No, never in your words,' she said,
'But in another way,
You've changed and that is set in stone
Whatever you may say.

'And with a heart so full of love
For who you were before,
I say our love is over now.'
She made towards the door.

Her parting words were sad indeed,
'Perhaps you'll feel some pain,
But only for the briefest time
Then you'll be right as rain.

'You'll think our love a waste of time
For it will surely seem,
As if it were a figment of
A brief and silly dream.'

She stood there for a moment,
Her whole being frozen.
She said, 'May you be happy in
The selfish life you've chosen.'

And that is how she left him –
They parted then forever.
Scrooge knew they never met again –
Not in the future – never!

'Ghost,' he cried, 'Show me no more.'
And then a fervent plea.
'Take me home I beg of you.
Why do you torture me?'

'One shadow more!' exclaimed the ghost.
Scrooge cried with trembling jaw,
'I do not wish to see it,
I beg you – show no more.'

But the Spirit was relentless
Though Scrooge was truly vexed.
He held his arms insisting
He watch what happened next.

WHAT MIGHT HAVE BEEN

And now another scene began,
A bright fire did illume
A small but warm and comfortable
And cosy sitting room.

Close to the roaring fire there sat
A lovely looking girl,
So like the last, that Scrooge's heart
Beat in a mighty whirl.

But when he looked again he saw
That she was with another –
And it was clear the matron there
Must be the young girl's mother.

Scrooge looked on and as he then
Rightly now suspected,
The mother was the lovely girl
That he had once rejected.

And also in the room that night
As Scrooge gazed sadly there
Were children playing all about –
Yes, children everywhere.

And all with laughing faces;
Oh, what a merry sight,
For everything was wonderful,
Just right and light and bright.

They rushed around, they made a noise,
They dodged behind a chair.
And all was quite beyond belief
But no-one seemed to care.

The mother and the daughter,
They both laughed heartily,
And now and then they'd pull a child
Up onto their knee.

And then a knocking sound was heard
Upon the outside door,
And when it opened Scrooge beheld
The father – and what's more…

He was accompanied by a man
Who thrilled the girls and boys,
For he was laden heavily
With presents and with toys.

The children rushed as one towards
The poor, defenceless porter;
They grabbed at parcels, presents and
They gave the man no quarter.

They searched inside his pockets,
They hung around his neck,
It would have been impossible
To hold them all in check.

And oh the joy and wonder
The grown-ups all perceived,
When they saw Christmas packages
So happily received.

The wrapping paper torn away
As if it were a race,
And then the sheer delight upon
A young and smiling face.

But finally it all was done
And so with nodding heads,
The children made their sleepy way
Up to their little beds.

Scrooge looked with interest as he saw
The master of the house
Sit quietly with his daughter
And his beloved spouse.

The daughter gazed into his eyes
With love she couldn't hide.
The mother too sat happily –
All by the fireside.

When Scrooge observed the lovely girl
Curl up against her father,
He felt regret and inwardly
He got into a lather.

To think a being of such grace
And full of promise too,
Might just have called him father if
He'd had a different view.

If he had made the mother there
His own beloved wife,
A daughter could have brought spring to
His haggard, winter life.

The husband then turned to his spouse
And had these words to say;
'Belle, I saw a long lost friend
Of yours, in town today.'

'Who was it?' she then asked of him.
'Why have a guess,' he said.
'How can I?' she replied – he laughed
And then threw back his head.

'Why it was Mr Scrooge, I passed
By his old place today.
I saw him through the window and
I am most sad to say…

'Although his partner lies right now
Very close to death,
And even as we speak he may
Have drawn his final breath…

'Old Scrooge sits in his Counting House,
Bent over – on his own
With not a friend in all the world –
He sits there all alone.'

Pained Scrooge looked now with furrowed brow
And rumpled, crumbling face.
'Ghost,' he cried in broken voice,
'Remove me from this place.'

The Spirit said, 'Do not blame me
For everything you've seen,
I told you these are shadows
Of things that once have been.'

'Remove me Spirit,' Scrooge implored.
'I cannot bear to stay.
Haunt me no longer – lead me back,
Oh please take me away.'

Scrooge, overcome with drowsiness
And exhaustion said,
'Spare me,' – then he was convinced
That he was back in bed.

And yes he was and gratefully,
Without another peep,
He sank beneath the blankets and
Was quickly fast asleep.

THE SECOND OF THE THREE SPIRITS

Scrooge woke up – he was right in
The middle of a snore.
At first his thoughts were muddled and
He really felt unsure.

He didn't know what time it was
But knew things must be done,
For surely now the time was close
To coming up to one.

He thought he'd regained consciousness
Right in the nick of time,
Just before the old church clock
Would resolutely chime…

The hour as being one o'clock,
And then he knew for sure,
The second of the Spirits would
Come floating through the door;

Or maybe through the wall – it made
No difference at all,
One thing was certain though, a ghost
Would surely come to call.

He drew the curtains of his bed
Cautiously aside,
So he would see immediately –
Across the great divide…

The moment that the ghost appeared,
With his poor, weary eyes.
He didn't wish to be caught out
Or taken by surprise.

And then the hour of one struck loud
Reverberating through
The gloomy house and Scrooge prepared
For his next interview.

But when no ghost appeared old Scrooge
Shook from head to toe,
As he sat waiting nervously
For some *thing* to show.

Five minutes past the hour went by,
Then ten and then the chime
To say it was now quarter past –
And during all this time…

He lay upon his meagre bed
Bathed in a ruddy light
Which had appeared at one o'clock –
And this alarming sight…

Caused him more consternation
Than several ghosts – and more,
And then he thought the light came from
Beneath his bedroom door.

This notion now possessed him,
The light came from, for sure,
The room adjoining his – he rose
And walked towards the door.

He shuffled in his slippers
And nervously took stock
Of all around and then he grasped
The key within the lock.

The moment that he did it
He heard a strange voice boom.
It called his name and bade him then
To come into the room.

And so he did as he was bid,
He turned the rusty key,
And as he did he wondered just
What in the world he'd see.

On entering, he looked around,
And what a great surprise,
It was his room and yet old Scrooge
Could not believe his eyes.

For it had surely undergone
A transformation there,
And all poor Scrooge could do was stand
With open mouth and stare.

The walls were hung with living green –
However did they grow?
For there was ivy – holly too
And gleaming mistletoe.

And mirrors too adorned the room
Reflecting back the light,
And what a roaring fire now blazed –
A warm and cheering sight.

And honestly it must be said
Old Scrooge was most amazed,
For never in the past had such
A massive fire blazed.

At least not in *his* dismal home –
But now he looked some more
And he could not believe just what
He saw piled on the floor.

For there was poultry – game as well,
And chunky joints of meat,
And with them keeping company
Was every kind of treat.

Tubs of oysters – chestnuts too,
Oranges and pears,
Just everything to satisfy
A gourmet's fervent prayers.

Plum pudding there and Christmas cake,
And lots of nuts to munch.
To top it all a steaming bowl
Of aromatic punch.

And there amidst the feast there sat –
Happy and defiant,
With torch in hand and smiling too –
A massive, jolly giant.

'Come in. Come in,' the ghost called out,
'Let's get acquainted,' – so
Scrooge entered very cautiously
And with his head bent low.

He couldn't bring himself to look
This Spirit in the eye.
For he was filled with awkwardness
And couldn't fathom why.

And yet the Spirit's eyes were clear,
They sparkled like a gem,
And they were kind but still old Scrooge
Could not look back at them.

'I am the Ghost,' the Spirit said,
'Of Christmas Present, so
Come look on me.' – Scrooge reverently,
With movements that were slow…

Looked up and viewed the Spirit;
It wore a robe of green,
Bordered with the whitest fur
That Scrooge had ever seen.

A wreath of holly crowned its head
And wildly hanging down
Were matted locks of curling hair
Of deepest, darkest brown.

Around its waist a scabbard hung,
But with no sword inside.
The ancient sheath was rusty but
The ghost wore it with pride.

To top it all this festive ghost
Had such a genial face,
A cheery voice, a sparkling eye,
An air of joy and grace.

It said, 'I'm sure you've never seen
The likes of me before.'
'Never in my life,' Scrooge breathed.
'Why Spirit, are there more?'

'Why yes, I've many brothers.'
His tone was warm and nice.
'More than eighteen hundred if
I am to be precise.'

Old Scrooge was open-mouthed – he said,
'Amazing – to be sure.'
The Ghost of Christmas Present rose
And motioned to the door.

'Take me where you will,' Scrooge sighed.
'I went abroad last night,
And I was shown the difference
'Twixt doing wrong and right.

'If you have lessons I should learn
Then lead me on I pray.'
'Touch my robe,' the ghost replied,
'And I will show the way.'

Scrooge did as he was told and then
The turkeys and the pies,
The holly and the mistletoe
Dissolved before his eyes.

The berries and the ivy,
The geese and poultry too,
The oysters and the sausages
All disappeared from view.

The pigs and meat and pudding,
The whole great, tasty stash,
Along with fruit and warming punch
Were gone in just a flash.

So did the room as well – for now
In less than one heart beat,
They found themselves on Christmas morn
Out in the city street.

BOB CRATCHIT'S CHRISTMAS

The weather was severe, thick snow
Had fallen everywhere;
It was a gloomy atmosphere
That seemed to linger there.

The sky above was cloudy,
The house fronts grimy grey,
A clinging mist lay all around
And shaped a dismal day.

So there was nothing cheerful
In the weather or the town;
There surely was good reason
For folk to wear a frown.

And yet an air of cheerfulness
Pervaded everywhere,
The people all seemed jovial
And free from any care.

They cleared the snow with shovels
And did it joyfully;
They talked and threw soft snowballs
And did it all with glee.

The way they laughed and carried on
Made such a happy story –
With shops so brightly lit that they
Were radiant in their glory.

Oh what a blissful Christmas scene
With not the slightest trace
Of selfishness – for kindliness
Lit everybody's face.

And then the Spirit led Scrooge to
A wretched part of town;
They went through streets that anxious Scrooge
Had seldom wandered down.

And now they reached Bob Cratchit's house,
All tumbledown and grey.
Bob was the clerk who laboured for
Old Scrooge each lifelong day.

Yes, decent Bob, the very same
Who Scrooge tried not to pay,
For having the temerity
For wanting Christmas Day…

To spend with his dear family –
Not very much to ask,
To have just one day off to be
Free from his daily task.

Now Scrooge looked on and there he saw
As he gazed mutely down,
Mrs Cratchit – Bob's dear wife
Dressed in a threadbare gown.

Her children were there with her,
Belinda – Peter too,
And they were cooking at the stove
As helpful children do.

'Where's father?' Mrs Cratchit asked.
'What has become of him?
And your sweet brother – where is he,
Our lovely Tiny Tim?

'And Martha wasn't late like this,
Not on last Christmas Day.
I hope she'll be here soon – let's hope
That she's now on her way.'

But then a cry went up and from
The children – they all cheered,
For Martha who they wished to see
Had suddenly appeared.

'Why bless your heart, how late you are,'
Good Mrs Cratchit said.
'I've worked so hard,' young Martha sighed,
'In truth, I feel half dead.'

'Well never mind, you're here my dear
So sit down by the fire,
And just relax and warm yourself
And to your heart's desire.'

'No, no,' the children cried out loud.
'Martha – you must hide,
For father's coming – don't sit down,
Not by the fireside.

'"Twould be such fun if you now found
A secret place and hid.'
So Martha very patiently
Did as her siblings bid.

The moment she was hidden
The door flew open wide;
Bob Cratchit entered joyfully
With one enormous stride.

Around his neck he wore a scarf,
His threadbare clothes were brushed.
He smiled and looked around and now,
The children were all hushed.

Upon Bob's shoulder rode a child,
And this was Tiny Tim,
And in his hand he held a crutch
Which swung in front of him.

One leg was in an iron frame,
A sorry sight indeed.
'Why, where's our Martha?' Bob cried out.
The children took no heed.

But Mrs Cratchit answered him.
'Not coming dear,' she said.
'Not coming here on Christmas Day?'
Bob turned a shade of red.

Martha saw he was upset
So sprang from where she lay,
She threw her arms around his waist –
'I'd not miss Christmas Day.'

Bob hugged his daughter gratefully
For all the love she gave,
Then Mrs Cratchit asked her spouse
'How did our Tim behave?'

Bob placed young Tim down gently
And patted his sweet head.
Tim shuffled off and Bob just smiled
And to his wife he said…

'As good as gold and better.'
Then soulfully he sighed.
'He quietly and happily
Remained right by my side.'

Then cheery Bob turned up his cuffs
And mixed a warming punch
That they would drink to liven up
Their festive Christmas lunch.

The happy children brought the goose,
Belinda made some sauce;
Their mother made hot gravy
And stirred her mash with force.

And Bob helped Tiny Tim to walk
As best as he was able,
To take his special place beside
His father at the table.

At last the meal was ready,
The children took their places;
You've never seen such joyful,
Glowing, happy faces.

Mrs Cratchit carved the goose,
Bob said it was by far
The finest goose he'd ever seen.
Tim feebly cried 'Hurrah.'

They all said grace and finally
The family were let loose
To then devour that succulent
And tasty Christmas goose.

They ate it up and all the way
Right to the very bone,
Then Bob's good wife got up and left
The humble room alone.

For she was apprehensive,
Nervous – in a fluff.
She'd gone to check the pud – suppose
It wasn't done enough.

Or maybe it would break apart,
But when she looked, she saw
That everything was perfect – yes,
Of that she was quite sure.

It speckled like a cannon ball,
The brandy on it blazed,
And when the children saw it
They truly were amazed.

For it was rich and wonderful,
With holly on the top.
'This pudding's better,' Bob cried out,
'Than any from a shop.'

He said, 'This is the tastiest
Dear wife, you've ever done.'
His wife confessed, 'I must admit
I fretted 'bout this one.

'I worried if I'd sprinkled in
The right amount of flour,
And if it would turn out to be
Too sweet or then too sour.'

They all said it was perfect –
Oh how they were in thrall,
And nobody suggested that
The pudding was too small.

For small it was – and yet for them
It was just such a prize,
No Cratchit would have ever thought
To comment on the size.

To do it would have made them blush,
They were just grateful for
The lovely pud and wouldn't think
To ever want for more.

THE FOUNDER OF THE FEAST

At last the dinner was all done,
The cloth was cleared away,
The hearth was swept – the fire made,
Then Bob was heard to say…

'A Merry Christmas, to us all.'
'God bless us,' they replied.
'God bless us. Every one,' called Tim.
Bob smiled there at his side.

He held his withered little hand,
How he loved Tiny Tim,
And how he dreaded that one day
He might be wrenched from him.

Scrooge now spoke, as he looked on,
In tone both sad and plaintive.
'Tell me Spirit – tell me please
If Tiny Tim will live?'

The Ghost looked down and then replied,
'I see a vacant seat
In the chimney corner and
Leant on the wall – so neat…

'A crutch without an owner,
So carefully preserved.
If these shadows stay like this,'
The Spirit then observed…

'The little child will surely die.'
Scrooge cried, 'Kind Spirit – no!
Please say he will be spared and that
He will then thrive and grow.'

'If these shadows stay as thus,
I tell you once again,
The future will be as it is
And so it shall remain.

'If he be like to die – well then
Nothing in creation
Can change it, so it's best if he
Decrease the population.'

Scrooge hung his head in penitence,
Ashamed of his own name,
To hear his own words quoted back,
(They were the very same)…

Was really awful – terrible –
And quite beyond belief.
He shuffled round uncomfortably
In sorrow and in grief.

The Ghost continued, for he said
With a resounding sigh,
'Will you decide which men should live
And also those that die?'

Scrooge bent before the Ghost's rebuke,
His eyes upon the ground
But raised them quickly when he heard
An unexpected sound.

It was somebody speaking and
They spoke his very name.
He heard the words – yes – 'Mr. Scrooge.'
Was this some kind of game?

But no it was Bob Cratchit's voice.
This was no subterfuge.
'Mr. Scrooge,' Bob cried aloud.
'I give you Mr. Scrooge.

'For he's the Founder of this Feast.'
Bob spoke with such good cheer.
His wife said, 'Founder of the Feast!
I wish I had him here.

'I'd give him something – that's for sure,
That he could feast upon.'
And as she spoke her face grew red –
All pleasantness was gone.

'I hope he'd have an appetite
For all I had to say.'
'My dear,' Bob said, 'the children!
And it *is* Christmas Day.'

'It should be Christmas Day,' she cried,
Words tumbling as they ran.
'To drink the health of such a hard,
Unfeeling kind of man.

'You know he is – for no-one knows
As well as you – I say.'
'My dear,' Bob answered once again,
'Remember – Christmas Day!'

Mrs Cratchit said, 'All right.
For you – I'll drink his health.
But still he'll celebrate alone
Despite his massive wealth.

'But for the day – long life to him –
I say it for you dear,
And so a merry Christmas Scrooge,
And happiness next year.'

The children drank the toast as well.
Tim drank it last of all.
He didn't care too much for it,
His voice was weak and small,

For in his mind old Scrooge was just
An ogre – for he'd cast
A shadow on the family
So often in the past.

The very mention of his name
Changed them from feeling hearty,
Into a group borne down, subdued –
To not a happy party.

But soon they all recovered
And merriment returned,
They stoked the fire – reluctantly
The meagre logs there burned.

They talked together happily,
Their old clock ticked along,
And then their little Tiny Tim
Sang a plaintive song.

All about a small, lost child
Travelling in the snow,
Frightened and bewildered for
He knew not where to go.

It was a sorry story
That Tim had there to tell,
He sang it through with feeling
And did it very well.

So there the Cratchit family
Enjoyed their Christmas Day,
Together with such joyfulness
In their own special way.

They weren't a handsome family,
And not well dressed, it's true.
Their shabby shoes weren't waterproof,
Their clothes were threadbare too.

But they were grateful, satisfied,
Content with one another;
They loved their daughter, sister, dad,
Their mother, son and brother.

And then the shadows faded
For it was time to go,
Scrooge had his eyes on all of them
Until the last – and so…

He watched them as they disappeared,
They fascinated him,
But most of all his eyes were on
Poor little Tiny Tim.

SCROOGE'S CHRISTMAS JOURNEY

It was now getting very dark
And snowing heavily,
And as they went along the streets
Scrooge could with ease then see…

The warming glow of roaring fires –
So colourful and bright.
In kitchens, parlours – everywhere,
A wondrous, joyful sight.

The flickering of candles,
The Christmas decorations,
Red curtains ready to be drawn –
All kinds of preparations.

Hot plates warming by the fire;
Christmas guests assembling.
Handsome girls in hoods and boots,
And all of them resembling…

Artful witches – woe upon
An unsuspecting man
Who saw them – for they would entrance
As only ladies can.

Then with no warning from the Ghost
Bewildered Scrooge now saw
The scene had altered once again –
They stood upon a moor.

It was deserted and quite bleak
And monstrous piles of stones
Lay all about – a blustery wind
Blew with loud moans and groans.

It looked just like the burial place
Of giants, long since dead,
So dark where desolation reigned.
'What place is this?' Scrooge said.

The Ghost replied, 'It is a place
Where miners live and toil.
They labour in the earth's deep bowels –
They burrow in the soil.'

He motioned then towards a hut
From which a small light shone;
He indicated to old Scrooge
That they should hurry on.

They made their way towards the hut
And passed right through its wall;
A fire was burning in the hearth
Which glowed, but was quite small;

And round it sat a company,
Warming by the fire,
All decked out and gaily in
Their holiday attire.

An old man and his wife were there,
Their children with them too,
Their children's children also –
A jolly family do.

Really quite a hearty throng,
A truly happy thing,
And then the old man croakily
Began, with zest, to sing.

They all joined in the chorus:
They sang with merry cheer:
The Ghost then said, 'Come hold my robe,
For we'll not tarry here.'

They left the moor – then horror,
This really couldn't be.
Scrooge fearfully looked down and saw
They now flew out to sea.

He saw the land was vanishing.
He really was in shock.
He saw the water thundering
And smashing onto rock.

And then a league or so off shore,
As mighty winds there blew,
A solitary lighthouse
Came into Scrooge's view.

It was as solid as a rock,
As strong as it could be,
There to help all threatened souls
Out on the raging sea.

'Twas built upon a dismal reef
Where giant seabirds flew,
Where waters chafed and dashed and crashed,
The whole wild, wet year through.

And in the lighthouse sat two men
Engulfed in sea and smog,
And each together raised his mug
Of alcoholic grog.

Their gnarled, rough hands were joined and each
Wished the other one
A Merry Christmas – and then once
Their greetings were all done,

They raised their voices manfully
And sang a sturdy song;
Their voices rang above the storm,
Loud, raucously and strong.

Again the Ghost sped on – he left
The lighthouse speedily;
On and on he went across
The black and heaving sea.

They left the reef, Scrooge held on tight
With nervous, clinging grip,
Till finally they lighted on
A rugged, sailing ship.

They stood beside the helmsman
Who tightly gripped the wheel –
Then by the lookout in the bow –
And then right by the heel…

Of the officer on watch;
Such ghostly figures who
Hummed a Christmas tune or had
A festive thought or two;

Or sometimes spoke beneath their breath
In a nostalgic way
Of revelry enjoyed upon
A previous Christmas Day.

And every man aboard the ship
Showed kindliness and cheer,
More than on any other day
Throughout the whole long year.

Rapt Scrooge stood there and heard the wind
Blow, bellow, fall and rise,
And then he heard a hearty laugh
Which came as a surprise.

And it was even greater when
He recognised the sound,
As being – yes – his nephew's voice,
And how it did resound…

Around the room where they now stood,
All gleaming, bright and dry.
The Spirit looked on affably
With humour in his eye.

He obviously approved of all
He saw before him there,
Especially of the nephew who
Sat chortling in a chair.

'Ha, ha,' he laughed. 'Ha, ha,' again.
No-one, by even half
Could e'er compete with such pure joy,
With such a happy laugh.

And it is surely true indeed
There's nothing in the world,
Quite as contagious as the sound
Of laughter when unfurled.

Then Scrooge's niece by marriage
Laughed heartily as well,
And their assembled friends all roared,
Caught by the selfsame spell.

Scrooge's nephew laughed some more.
He cried, 'I'm telling you,
He said, "Humbug to Christmas."
And he believes it too.'

Scrooge's niece said, 'Shame on him.'
Her husband then replied,
'Oh, he's a funny fellow;
It's true – I've never lied.

'He's not as pleasant as I'm sure
He really ought to be,
But that brings its own punishment
As we can clearly see.'

'I'm sure he's rich,' his wife went on.
'At least Fred, so you say.'
'What of it though, my dear?' Fred said,
'For there is just no way…

'His wealth does any good at all,
For him, or anyone,
He gets no comfort – benefit –
When all is said and done.'

'I have no patience with him,'
His wife said angrily.
The others there agreed as well
But Fred said, 'Let it be.

'I'm sorry for the fellow so
I can't get cross with him.
Who suffers by his awkwardness
Or each obnoxious whim?

'Why Scrooge himself – it is his right,
We should not cause a fuss
If he decides he will not come
For Christmas lunch with us.

'But I'm convinced that by this choice
He misses out for sure
On many pleasant moments and
He could have countless more,

'If he would only change his ways –
And I mean for my part,
To try to warm his attitude
And melt his stony heart.

'And so at every Christmas time
Though he'd have it forgot,
I do intend to ask him here,
Like it or like it not.'

The company all laughed out loud
Then passed the bottle round,
And as they spoke and laughed it was
A happy Christmas sound.

They played light music after tea,
And then they played some games –
All sorts of joyful pastimes
With funny sounding names.

Like Forfeits, which was very good,
And Blind Man's Bluff as well.
The games made everybody laugh
And brought them from their shell.

And as the playfulness increased,
And strange as it may seem,
Old Scrooge became quite overcome
Though it was but a dream.

For when they played How, When and Where,
He found he must join in,
And shouted out his answers
Above the rising din.

Of course he quite ignored the fact
That he could not be heard,
He was but a spectator
To things as they occurred.

But still he called his answers out –
Oh what a happy sight,
For most of Scrooge's guesses
Turned out to be quite right.

The Ghost was very pleased to see
Old Scrooge in such a mood,
'Twas quite a change from seeing him
  A selfish wretch and rude.

There was no stopping Scrooge now that
His pleasantness had started,
He wished to stay right up until
The last guest had departed.

But the Spirit was insistent
That this could not be done,
Though Scrooge protested massively
That he was having fun.

'Here's a new game,' Scrooge cried out.
'Oh just a half hour more.'
And so they listened while young Fred,
Alone – took to the floor.

It was a game called 'Yes and No'.
Fred thought of something – then
The others had to find it out
By asking, 'What or When…

'Or How – or is it something that
We see a lot or know?'
Whatever question asked of Fred,
He cried just 'Yes' or 'No'.

By asking many questions
They finally found out,
It was an animal – and then
There was another shout.

Was it a savage creature
That growled and grunted too?
Fred replied and with a 'Yes'
And now there was a queue.

And how they jostled and all joked
To get their question in;
You should have heard their laughter –
Such a cheerful din.

For all there had a question.
'Does it live in a zoo?'
Or 'Is it killed at market?'
Then someone cried they knew.

It was the niece's sister,
All plump and fat and round.
She cried, 'I know the answer Fred.'
And laughter did resound…

Around the room – what jollity –
Dear Fred, he laughed out loud,
The sister yelled her answer
Above the boisterous crowd.

'It is your Uncle Scrooge,' she cried.
And Fred said, 'Yes, that's right.'
And everybody fell about
As indeed they might.

Then Fred said, 'As he's given us
Such merriment today,
It would be most ungrateful if
We failed to stand and say…

'A thank you to my Uncle Scrooge –
Though stingy with his wealth –
And mean and moody – miserable –
But friends – let's toast his health.'

'To Uncle Scrooge,' they cried as one
And Fred went on to say,
'A Merry Christmas Uncle
Despite your awful way.

'A Happy New Year to you too
Although it's clear to see,
You wouldn't want it anyway
Because it comes from me.'

Scrooge looking on had now become
All gay and light and bright,
For never in his life had he
Seen such a warming sight.

Indeed he wished to thank them
For drinking such a toast,
But in an instant he was whisked,
By the impatient Ghost…

Off on their travels once again;
The last thing that he heard
Was his young nephew speaking and
The breath of his last word.

A LONG AND WEARY NIGHT

That night they saw so many things,
Just how a faithful friend
Could aid someone who needed help
And bring a happy end.

They stood by sick beds, where they saw
Adversity was near;
So many who were ill fought on
With fortitude and cheer.

How struggling men showed patience
And lived with fervent hope
That somehow 'gainst great poverty
They'd find a way to cope.

In almshouses and hospitals,
In jails, and everywhere
That misery resided,
The Spirit took great care.

It left a heartfelt blessing for
The lost, the poor, the lame,
And it taught Scrooge most carefully
That he should do the same.

It was a long and weary night,
Indeed was it just one?
Scrooge had his doubts because it seemed
Far more when it was done.

And as they journeyed on – the night
Grew frosty and much colder;
Scrooge observed the Spirit there
Was clearly growing older.

He'd noticed this before, but now
He was inclined to say,
Because he clearly saw the Ghost
Was turning almost grey,

'Are Spirits lives so short?' he asked,
For time seemed such a thief.
The Spirit sighed and he replied,
'My life is very brief.

'My time upon this globe will end
Upon this very night.'
'Tonight?' cried Scrooge – he shuddered then
With overpowering fright.

'Yes,' the Ghost replied. 'And soon!
At midnight's hour, I fear;
And hark the chimes are ringing out,
The time is drawing near.

'The chimes now ring and tell the hour,
Three quarters past eleven.
My life will soon be over for
It is the will of heaven.'

Then from the folding of its robe
Scrooge was amazed to see,
Two little waifs emerge, they stood
Cowering miserably.

And they were wretched, abject, lost,
A little girl and boy,
Quite hideous and miserable,
Devoid of any joy.

Yellow, meagre, scowling,
They also seemed to be
Borne down and prostrate deep within –
In their humility.

Scrooge started back – he was appalled
To see them in this way.
As he looked on in horror
He tried so hard to say…

That they were lovely children,
Of very special note,
Quite fine in every way – but then
The words stuck in his throat.

For even he could not give voice
To such a massive lie.
'Spirit, are they yours?' he asked
And with a heavy sigh.

The Spirit said, 'No, they are Man's,
But still they cling to me.
For they are Ignorance and Want
And they will always be…

'Unless the Doom that's writ upon
Their brows is thus erased.'
And then the Spirit turned so that
His countenance now gazed…

Towards the city – then he stretched
His hand and cried out loud,
'Deny this if you can but there,
Within the city's crowd…

'There lies the stark reality.'
It startled frightened Scrooge.
He said, 'What can the children do?
Is there no safe refuge?'

The Spirit said, 'Well, some do say
The Workhouse – it will do.'
Scrooge recognised the Spirit's words –
They were his own, he knew.

And then the clock struck twelve and as
Unhappy Scrooge looked on,
He realised the second Ghost
Had disappeared and gone.

And as the final stroke rang out,
Vibrating through the air,
And as bewildered Scrooge just stood,
Alone and shaking there…

He thought of Jacob Marley
And everything he'd said,
And once again his being was
Filled with a clinging dread.

Then lifting up his eyes he saw –
Not far from where he stood –
A solemn Phantom, draped and in
A sombre looking hood.

And though the night was inky dark –
The light was very dim,
He saw it floating like a mist,
Along the ground – to him!

THE LAST OF THE SPIRITS

The Phantom now approaching moved
With solemn gravity:
It came in silence, slowly too.
Scrooge dropped onto one knee…

For as it moved the Spirit seemed
To cause the very air
To scatter gloom and mystery
Around it – everywhere.

'Twas shrouded in a garment
Of deepest, darkest black;
Concealing everything, it draped
In straight folds down its back.

Impossible for Scrooge to see
Even the slightest trace –
Against the blackness of the night –
Of form or head or face.

The apparition blended there
As it took sombre stand,
With nothing visible at all
Except one outstretched hand.

When it came up beside him
Old Scrooge was filled with dread;
The Spirit neither spoke nor moved:
Scrooge finally then said…

'I'm in the presence of the Ghost
Of Christmas yet to Come?'
No answer came and thus it seemed
As if the Ghost were dumb.

It pointed onward with its hand.
Unmoving – rigid – set.
Scrooge said, 'You've come to show me things
That haven't happened yet.

'Shadows of the things to come.
Spirit – is that so?'
The Spirit uttered not a word,
Neither a 'Yes' or 'No'.

But the shrouded hood it wore
Then seemed to fold instead,
As if to indicate the Ghost
Had just inclined its head.

This was its only gesture –
Scrooge wished he could escape,
For though now used to Spirits
He feared this silent shape.

His legs trembled there beneath him
And he could barely stand;
The Spirit paused – a great, black shape
With just that outstretched hand.

It let poor Scrooge recover,
But he was filled with fear,
To think behind the dusky shroud,
And standing there so near…

Two ghostly eyes were fixed on him –
But when scared Scrooge looked back,
He saw but just that spectral hand
And one great heap of black.

'Ghost of the Future,' Scrooge exclaimed,
'I fear you in your hood,
More than the others I have seen
Though you're here for my good.

'I hope to live to now become
A changed man from before,
So I'm prepared to follow you
And see all you've in store.

'And I will do it willingly
And with a grateful heart,
But Spirit will you speak to me
Before we make our start?'

The Spirit gave him no reply
But pointed with its hand.
Scrooge cried, 'Lead on, lead on, for I
Do fully understand…

'The night is moving on – and yes
It's precious time I know,
So lead on Spirit, quickly now –
I'll follow where you go.'

THE WRETCH IS DEAD

The Phantom moved away and Scrooge,
With some degree of dread,
Found himself borne up and he
Now followed where it led.

Then suddenly they found themselves
In a city street,
Right in its heart – and on a road
Where merchants chose to meet.

They hurried up and down and talked
In little groups and then
Looked at their watches to imply
That they were busy men.

They chinked coins in their pockets;
They all seemed bright and keen.
This was the normal tapestry
That Scrooge had often seen.

The Spirit stopped right there beside
A huddled group of men,
Scrooge advanced to overhear
Their conversation when…

He heard a fat man with a chin –
Quite monstrous – who then said,
'I don't know much about it but
I do know that he's dead.'

'When did he die?' another asked,
Standing to the right.
'From what I've heard, I do believe
It was some time last night.'

'What was the cause?' a third one asked,
And gave a little sigh,
And took a pinch of snuff and laughed,
'I thought he'd never die.'

'God knows,' the first replied and yawned.
A red-faced man then said,
'What happens now to all his cash,
Now that the wretch is dead?'

'I haven't heard,' the large chinned man
Said sighing massively.
'Although one thing, I know for sure,
It's not been left to me!'

At this, the gathering all laughed –
'Also,' he said, 'for sure,
The funeral's likely to be cheap,
The man was such a bore.

'And I would state with certainty,
I really do not know
Of anyone, who'd willingly,
Make the choice to go.'

'But we could make a party up,'
Another man then said.
'I don't mind going but insist
I must be amply fed.

'A lunch must be provided.'
Which caused a further laugh.
A thin man said, 'I never wear
Black gloves or charcoal scarf.

'Or indeed eat lunch at all,
But maybe, even still,
I will agree to be there if
Some of you also will.

'In fact now that I think of it,
Most likely it was I
Who knew him best, for when we met
We'd speak as we passed by.'

The group broke up and strolled away.
Scrooge stood wracked with vexation.
He looked towards the Spirit
To seek an explanation.

The Phantom glided onwards,
Its finger pointing, then
Scrooge saw that he was looking at
Two chatting gentlemen.

Scrooge knew them as he'd also known
The others they had seen.
For they were men of business
And both had always been…

Renowned for their importance
And wealth – they stood supreme
Within the town and Scrooge thought he
Stood high in their esteem.

'How are you?' asked one gentleman.
'I'm very well today.'
The first one said, 'It seems old Scratch
Got his at last – what hey!'

The second rubbed his hands and said,
'Oh yes, so I've been told.'
And then he stamped his feet and moaned,
'My word, it has turned cold.'

'Seasonably for Christmas time,'
The other man replied.
'Good morning to you.' Nothing more
Was said of he who'd died.

They parted with no further word
And Scrooge was most surprised.
Why was the Ghost so keen he see
These men – he then surmised…

There was a lesson to be learned
So now he sought to see,
The meaning in their trivial talk.
Whatever could it be?

However much he wracked his brain,
He couldn't work it out.
He really couldn't fathom what
The whole thing was about.

He peered again towards the crowd
To look upon the spot
Where generally he took his place.
Would he be there or not?

There was no sign of Scrooge himself,
Then he became aware
Of the Phantom by his side,
Just calmly standing there.

And he was certain, right beneath
The charcoal hood's great fold,
The Spirit's unseen eyes looked down.
The knowledge turned Scrooge cold.

A DISRESPECTFUL GATHERING

They left the busy scene and now
Took an obscure route,
To a part of town Scrooge knew
To be of ill repute.

The streets were foul and narrow,
The people poorly dressed;
Ugly, drunken – many were
Unhappy and distressed.

The shops and houses wretched,
Cesspools everywhere,
Disgorging smells and dirt and all –
Life here was so unfair.

The quarter reeked of misery,
Of filth and dirty slime,
And all along the struggling streets
There lurked all kinds of crime.

And in this heaving den of vice
There was a scruffy shop,
And it was here the Ghost now made
Another prolonged stop.

The shop was just a jumble
Of iron, bottles, chains;
Of rusty keys, of nails and weights –
And such ill-gotten gains.

And in amongst them all there sat
A grey-haired bent old man,
Who smoked his pipe contentedly
As only ancients can.

Scrooge and the Spirit had arrived
Just as a woman slunk
Into the shop – she seemed to have
A bundle full of junk.

And she had hardly entered
And said, 'How do ye do?'
When another woman came –
Similarly laden too.

And she was also followed by
A man dressed all in black,
And when the women saw him they
Seemed taken quite aback.

'Well here's a thing,' the first old hag
Said as she viewed them all.
'First the humble char – that's me,
Comes to make a call.

'Then the laundress comes as well
And then no other than –
By some amazing chance – here is
The undertaker's man.

'Well old Joe – now there's a thing,
It really is quite queer,
Whatever is the chance we'd all
Converge and end up here.

'Arriving here just at the time
The others come – I say
That this has not occurred before.
Well, not until today.'

Joe shook his pipe and tapped the bowl,
A smile lit up his face.
'Why none of you could choose to meet
In a nicer place.

'So come into the parlour now.'
They did as they were bid.
One woman said, 'Look to yourself,
Indeed – he always did.'

'That's true enough,' the laundress said,
'And not a man, more so.
He looked out for himself – that is
One thing I surely know.

'And so we'll not be hard upon
Each other – I suppose.'
'No, indeed,' the other said.
'We're all as one – God knows.'

And so in turn the three of them
Undid their bundles there;
They laid the contents out for Joe
And with the utmost care.

The undertaker's man went first
And set out on the floor,
Some seals, a pencil-case, a brooch –
There was but little more.

Old Joe did calculations
And said how much he'd pay.
He said, 'You'll not get any more
No matter what you say.'

Then a lady took her turn,
She laid her spoils down;
She waited while Joe sifted through,
Her face set in a frown.

Some sheets and towels were lying there,
Some silver teaspoons too,
Some sugar tongs and dirty boots.
Joe added up and drew…

A number on the wall to show
Just how much he'd pay.
And then he spoke to her and said
In a conniving way,

'My dear, there's your account, and if
You argue or you frown,
I'll kill my generosity
And knock off half a crown.

'I'm always far too generous
To ladies – I must say
That it will ruin me for sure
On some dire future day.'

'And now see to my bundle Joe,'
The other woman said.
'He'll have no use for all this stuff
Now that the old screw's dead.'

Joe fell onto his knees to look –
And found a heavy roll.
It looked liked curtains. He exclaimed,
'Bed curtains – bless my soul.'

The woman laughing, leaned across
And raised a pudgy arm,
She fluffed them up – 'Bed curtains – yes!
It can't do any harm.'

Joe said, 'You do not mean to say,'
He wore an awful stare,
'You took 'em down – the rings and all
With him still lying there?'

The woman gazed back brazenly.
'Yes I do,' she said.
'And why not for the misery
Was surely good and dead.'

'You were born to make your fortune,'
Joe said with savvy wit.
'The way you're acting will ensure
That you'll accomplish it!'

The woman's only comment –
'Just watch those blankets, Joe.
Don't drop that oil upon them.
Be careful how you go.'

'His blankets?' Joe responded.
The woman didn't shrink.
'Of course they are,' she cried aloud.
'Whose else's do you think?

'He isn't likely to catch cold
Without them now, I'd say.
So come on Joe and tell me now –
How much will you pay?'

Joe stopped his work and pondered.
'I hope he didn't die
Of something catching.' She just laughed
And then said with a sigh,

'Don't be afraid of that at all,
I'm not so very fond
Of him who's now departed
Into the great beyond…

'That I would hang around and take
His things now, if he did.
Now then, take this shirt here Joe,
And say how much you'll bid,

'For it's not threadbare – not at all.
It was his best I'd say,
And they'd have wasted it, if Joe
They had had their way.'

'What do you mean by wasted?'
Joe asked her curiously.
The woman laughed and tossed her head
And clapped her hands with glee.

'Why putting it upon the wretch
To bury him,' she said.
'Someone placed it on him but
I took it off instead.'

Now Scrooge was listening to this
His senses all agog;
His eyes were blazing angrily
At this foul dialogue.

He thought the whole thing terrible,
Wicked and unjust,
He viewed them all with horror,
Annoyance and disgust.

Then a woman laughed when Joe
Gave her a bag of cash.
She grabbed it quickly – checked it,
Then hid it in a flash.

'He frightened everyone away
When he was still alive,
But now he's gone he'll profit us
And help us to survive.'

She laughed again and everyone
Happily joined in,
And soon their joyful mirth had caused
A tasteless, unfit din.

Scrooge looked towards the Spirit
And sadly shook his head;
'The case of this unhappy man –
It could be mine instead.

'For my life tends this way right now.'
Then 'What is this?' he cried,
As he stepped back in terror
Jaw dropping and wide-eyed.

For once again the scene had changed.
Wherever could he be?
Confusion coursed through Scrooge's mind
As he tried hard to see.

THE MOTION OF A FINGER

And then before him he perceived
A bare, uncurtained bed,
And lying there beneath a sheet
To fill his mind with dread…

Was something covered up – it was
Nothing other than
An awful, sombre, wretched shape –
The body of a man.

It lay there plundered and bereft,
Unwatched o'er – all alone,
Unwept for and uncared for,
Just left there on its own.

Scrooge glanced towards the Phantom,
He saw its mournful hand
Now pointed at the dead man's head,
To make Scrooge understand…

Some awful lesson, but all Scrooge
Saw as his eyes cast down,
Was a cover ruffled there
Exposing the man's crown.

The motion of a finger
By just the slightest trace
On Scrooge's part – would deftly have
Revealed the dead man's face.

Scrooge thought about how easy
'Twould be for him to do,
But had no inclination
To take a furtive view.

But as he looked he wondered
If raised now from the dead,
Would greedy thoughts be uppermost
Within the poor man's head?

Would griping cares and avarice
Be his initial feeling?
Followed by a burning urge
To carry on hard dealing.

For now the man lay in the house
And from what Scrooge was seeing,
Devoid of any kindness from
Another human being.

There was a scraping at the door,
But it was just the cat,
And gnawing at the hearthstone
Could only be a rat.

Their presence in this dismal room
Made frightened Scrooge there shrink;
Why they were restless and disturbed
Scrooge did not dare to think.

'Dark Spirit,' he declared, 'I feel
This is a fearful place,
And I do solemnly avow
That such will be the case…

'That when we leave, I will retain
Its lesson and will show
That it has changed me – now, please Ghost,
Let's flee from here – let's go!'

But still the Spirit pointed
Its finger at the head.
'I understand you Spirit and,
Would do it,' Scrooge then said.

'But I don't have the nerve to look.'
The Spirit stared at him,
An apparition dark and bleak,
Horrific and most grim.

'If there's a person,' Scrooge implored,
His face set in a frown,
'Who feels emotion by this death
Anywhere in town…

'Then show that person to me,
I humbly beg of you.'
He knew, of course, the Spirit could
If this – he chose to do.

A DEATH BRINGS SOME RELIEF

The Phantom spread its long, dark robe,
It looked just like a wing;
A massive, dark, enveloping
And eerie kind of thing.

When he withdrew it, Scrooge then saw
A charming, daylit room,
A contrast overwhelming from
The deathbed's musty gloom.

He saw children with their mother,
The mother paced the floor,
Starting at each sound she heard
And looking at the door.

She gazed out of the window
And looked towards the clock,
Till happily she heard at last
The long-expected knock.

Her husband entered then, his face
Was careworn though still young.
He sat down by the warming fire –
His coat was swiftly hung –

And then he looked at his dear wife,
And she enquired, 'What news?'
'Twas clear her consternation
Did overflow and ooze…

From every part of her slight frame –
Her face was tense and sad.
She spoke again with fearful voice,
'So is it good – or bad?'

'It's bad,' he said unhappily,
'But somehow we will cope.'
'We're ruined then,' she said – he sighed,
'There's still a little hope.'

'Why, may the wretched man relent?'
His nervous wife then said.
'He's past relenting,' came reply.
'For now the man is dead!'

His wife, a kindly creature
And mild in every way ,
Nonetheless was thankful
To hear her husband say…

The man was dead – but as she thought
This dreadful thought, she prayed
To be forgiven – her good side
Was quickly now displayed.

Her husband said, 'When just last week
I went along to say
I couldn't pay and wished to beg
A seven day delay…

'I found the house all shuttered,
It looked extremely bleak.
I didn't get to see the man
With whom I wished to speak.

'A drunken woman at the door,
Turned me, in haste, away
And said 'twas inconvenient
To see him on that day;

'And heaven knows, she told the truth,
For he was not just ill,
But dying – really quite beyond
A clever doctor's skill.'

His wife then said, 'So tell me dear
Now that this has occurred,
To whom in this whole sorry world
Will our debt be referred?'

'Well time will tell,' he said, 'but this
I think I know for sure,
He couldn't be as bad as he
Who squeezed the wretched poor.

'Of all the money lenders,
He really was the worst.
And everybody felt the same.
The man was widely cursed.

'And so tonight perhaps we may
Place our worried heads
Upon our pillows and my dear
Sleep lighter in our beds.'

Their children clustered round and though
They little understood,
They felt that something had occurred
Their parents thought was good.

Fraught Scrooge looked on with heavy heart
And heaving, gasping breath.
'Please let me see some tenderness
Connected with this death.

'Spirit, please,' he asked, 'I beg,
Or else I'll always see
That dark chamber – it will stay
Forever here with me.'

THE SHARPEST BLOW OF ALL

The Ghost conducted Scrooge through streets
That were well known to him.
He followed on – resigned to this,
The Ghost's new, fickle whim.

They entered then Bob Cratchit's house
Where Scrooge had been before,
And when they entered silently
Right through his run-down door…

They saw the Cratchit children
With their mother and they sat
By the fire – and sombrely;
The atmosphere was flat.

The noisy little Cratchits
Sat every one, quite still,
Like statues – it could almost seem
The children might be ill.

But this would be delusion
For it was not the case,
And then their mother put her hand
With tiredness to her face.

'Father should be home quite soon.
It must be near his time.'
'Past it rather,' Peter said.
'I heard the clock just chime.

'Poor father's walking slower now,'
Peter then observed.
'His manner too has changed a bit –
For he is more reserved.'

She replied, 'I've known him walk
Much faster – even though
He used to carry Tiny Tim –
But now his pace is slow.

'And I'm afraid that father
Is now looking older;
It gave him heart to feel dear Tim
Sitting on his shoulder,

'For Tim was light to carry
As all you children know,
It was no trouble for your dad
Because he loved him so.

'Ah, there, I hear him coming now.'
The mother said no more;
She hurried out to greet dear Bob
As he approached the door.

His tea was waiting there for him,
Kept warm upon the hob.
The children gathered round as if
They would console poor Bob.

But he was cheerful with them
In his most pleasant way.
And then his wife spoke up and said,
'You went there then, today?'

'Yes, my dear,' returned kind Bob.
His poor worn face looked wan.
'I've picked a green and lovely spot,
I wish you could have gone.

'But you will see it often.
I've promised him we'd walk
To see him every Sunday morn
And have a little talk.

'My little child. My little child.'
He broke down then and cried.
He left the room and went upstairs
To see his child who'd died.

He steeled himself to look upon
The one he loved so much.
He placed his hand upon the child's
With soft and gentle touch.

Tim was lying silently.
Bob sat down by his side.
Emotion overwhelmed him and
Distraught Bob Cratchit cried.

He thought awhile and then, composed,
He kissed Tim's little face.
The room was dressed for Christmas
Which lightened that sad place.

Then feeling somewhat better
Though still borne down with cares,
Bob made his solemn way back to
The fireside downstairs.

They drew their chairs together
And Bob began to tell,
How Mr Scrooge's nephew
Had treated him so well.

'I've only met him just the once
But saw him in the street.
And it was purely by a chance
We happened there to meet.

'He said he noticed I looked down.'
Bob coughed and gave a pause.
'He asked me if I were upset
And if so, what the cause?

'And when I told him, he replied
In such a concerned way,
"I'm truly most distressed, dear chap
To hear of this today."

'His manner was so gentle.
He spoke so kindly thus,
It seemed as if he knew our Tim
And felt for him with us.'

Scrooge wrestled with this tragic scene,
Then to the Ghost he said,
'I think our time is running short –
I must speak of the dead.

'Tell me, who did we behold
Lying dead before?'
The Ghost of Christmas Yet to Come
Looked down on Scrooge once more,

And then he hurried them away
To somewhere else he sought.
It was a place that Scrooge knew well,
It was the very court…

In which he had his business;
Scrooge said, 'This is the place
Wherein I work – just over there.'
The thought lit up his face.

'Let me behold what I shall be
In days to come, I pray.'
The Spirit's hand, now held aloft
Pointed the other way.

'The building's yonder,' Scrooge exclaimed.
'Why do you point elsewhere?'
He hurried to his office then
To see if *he* was there.

On looking through the window
Dismay coursed through his frame;
The furniture looked different
And nothing was the same.

The person seated in the chair
Beside an old bookshelf,
Was someone he had never seen –
And surely not himself.

The Phantom pointed yet again.
Scrooge joined the Ghost once more,
Wondering why he'd gone that way
And what now lay in store.

At last they reached an iron gate,
Scrooge looked to ascertain
Just where they were – and now once more
He was surprised again;

For when they pushed the dismal gate
Scrooge paused and looked around,
And saw it was a churchyard,
Where underneath the ground…

He guessed there lay the wretched man
Whose name he would now learn.
It seemed a dismal kind of place
From what he could discern.

Walled in by houses – overrun
With unkempt grass and weed –
Choked up with so much burying,
A worthy place indeed!

The Spirit stood among the graves,
Its night's work nearly done,
Motionless – it cast around,
Then pointed down at one.

Although the Phantom still remained
The same in hood and drape,
Scrooge thought he saw new meaning in
Its black and eerie shape.

'Before I now approach,' Scrooge spoke
With apprehensive ring.
'Unto the stone at which you point,
Ghost – answer me one thing.

'Are these shadows that *must* pass
Or shadows that *may* be?
Tell me, I beg, these things can change
That you have shown to me.'

But still the Spirit standing there
In its black, sombre gown,
Was quite immovable – it stood
With finger pointing down.

Scrooge crept toward it trembling –
Followed the finger to
The overgrown, neglected grave.
Its stone now filled his view.

And there upon that dismal stone
He saw his own sad name.
EBENEZER SCROOGE it read,
Oh yes, the very same.

He fell onto his knees and cried
In overpowering dread.
'Am I the man who lay upon
That dismal, lonely bed?'

The Spirit pointed to the grave
And back to him again.
Then to the grave – to Scrooge once more
To make it very plain…

That yes, he was the wretched man –
Scrooge wobbled to and fro,
In fearfulness he cried out loud,
'No Spirit! Oh, no, no!'

The finger pointed just the same.
Remorseless – like a probe.
'Hear me! Hear me!' Scrooge cried out
Clutching at its robe.

'I'm not the man I used to be.
I'll not slide down that slope.
Why do you show me all these things
If I am past all hope?'

The Phantom's hand appeared to shake.
Scrooge fell onto his knees.
The dismal graveyard was now filled
With Scrooge's fervent pleas.

'Spirit, pity me,' he cried.
'And tell me, now I've changed,
The shadows you have shown to me
Can all be rearranged.'

And then the Spirit's hand seemed kind.
Scrooge cried, 'I'll make fresh start,
And I will carry Christmas time
All year – within my heart.

'I'll live in Past and Present
And in the Future too.
And I'll do everything the Ghosts
Have taught me I should do.

'The Spirits of all Three shall thrive
Constantly in me,
I will not shut their lessons out –
I will be true – you'll see.

'So tell me I can still avoid
Dying on my own.
That I may sponge away somehow
The writing on the stone.'

In his agony he caught
The spectre by the hand,
He was determined that he'd make
The Spirit understand.

It sought to free itself, but Scrooge
Held on desperately,
But then the Ghost proved stronger
And finally broke free.

Scrooge held his hands aloft once more
In one last, desperate prayer,
And then the Phantom, hood and drape
Transformed as he stood there.

It shrank, collapsed and dwindled,
And then that sombre Ghost
Disappeared and then became
An every day bedpost!

CHRISTMAS MORNING

And yes – the bedpost was his own,
The bed his own as well,
And the room – but best of all
As far as Scrooge could tell,

The Time before him was his own
So he could make amends,
And change his ways and maybe too
Make himself some friends.

'I'll live in Past and Present,
The Future too,' he said,
Repeating all he'd vowed before,
As he leapt out of bed.

'The Spirits words will thrive in me.
Oh Jacob Marley, please,
Let Christmas Time be praised – for this
I vow upon my knees.'

He was so flustered and aglow
With good resolve and all,
That his hoarse, broken voice would not
Answer to his call.

For he was sobbing violently,
His face was wet with tears,
No longer now the selfish soul
Of all those former years.

He grabbed the old bed curtains
Hanging at his side.
'The rings are all in place as well,'
Exultantly he cried.

'They are here and I'm here too.'
The thought gave him a thrill.
'The shadows too may be dispelled,
And yes, I vow they will.'

He grabbed the garments lying there
And did his best to don
His outdoor clothes – but messed it up
In haste to get them on.

'I don't know what to do,' he cried,
Laughing out with joy.
'I'm happy like an angel,
And merry as a boy.

'I'm light as any feather.'
His happiness unfurled.
'As jolly as a drunken man.
Oh what a lovely world.'

He skipped into the sitting room
And there came into view,
The saucepan that had cooked his gruel,
And Scrooge cried, 'Yes, it's true.

'There's the door through which the Ghost
Of Jacob Marley came.
The Ghost of Christmas Present sat
Right there – the spot's the same.

'And there's the window where I saw
The wandering spirits fly,
So it's all right – it is all true.'
He cried with happy sigh.

And then he laughed out loud – it was
A truly splendid sound.
A joyous laugh considering
No laughter had been found…

In Scrooge's house for many years,
But now this burst of laughter –
Would be the first of many that
Would come forever after.

He danced around and then exclaimed,
'Whatever day is this?
I really don't know anything,
But everything is bliss.

'I've been amongst the Spirits
But how long was I there?
I'm quite a baby – that's for sure
But really – I don't care.

'I'd rather be a baby… '
But then he heard a thing
That made his heart beat very fast,
He heard the church bells ring.

And they rang out in such a way
He'd never known before;
Such lusty peals – so glorious,
They made his spirits soar.

Running to the window
He opened it to stare
Upon a day so clear and bright
And with such sweet, fresh air.

With golden sunlight streaming down,
It was all such a treat.
It lit the heavenly sky above
And brightened up the street.

Scrooge saw a little boy below
Who slowly made his way
Along the street – so Scrooge called down,
'What day is it today?'

The boy responded with a grunt.
So with a raucous bellow,
Scrooge called again with joyful tone,
'What's today, fine fellow?'

'Today!' the little boy replied
In such a startled way.
Then looking up he boldly cried,
'Why – it's Christmas Day!'

Scrooge was overjoyed – he felt
Relieved, borne up and light.
He thought the Spirits must have done
The whole thing in one night.

And then he thought again – 'Oh yes!
It's Christmas Day – oh joy!
I haven't missed it after all.'
And called down to the boy.

'Hallo – fine fellow – yes, you there.'
He'd never felt so glad.
'Now do you know the poulterer?'
'I do,' replied the lad.

'What intelligence,' Scrooge sighed.
'Remarkable for sure.
You know they have a turkey
Hanging by the door.

'The one that's quite enormous.
As large as one could be.'
The little boy replied, 'The one
That is as big as me?'

'What a charming boy,' Scrooge cried.
'It's such a stroke of luck
That you were passing by today –
Yes, that's the one, my buck.'

The boy replied, 'It's hanging there
Right now – I just walked by.'
'Well go and buy it for me please.'
The boy thought it a lie.

'You're joking,' he replied – Scrooge said –
'If you, my boy, are willing
To go and purchase it, well then
You'll earn yourself a shilling.

'Come back in just five minutes
For it's not far 'cross town,
And if you do – well my good lad
I'll give you half a crown.

'Ask the man to bring it here
So I can tell him where
I want the turkey taken,
Now off you go – take care.'

The boy shot off immediately.
Scrooge rubbed his hands with glee.
'I'll send it to Bob Cratchit's but
I'll not say it's from me.

'It's twice the size of Tiny Tim,
And then again by half.'
Scrooge thought it would be such a joke
And couldn't help but laugh.

He scribbled out poor Bob's address
With trembling, shaky hand,
Then made his way to his front door –
There to calmly stand…

Until the boy returned – but then
The knocker caught his eye.
'I'll love you,' he said patting it,
'Until the day I die.

'I scarcely looked at it before
But what an honest face.
A knocker that's quite wonderful,
This truly is the case.

'But hallo! Here's the turkey.
How are you there, good sir?
A Merry Christmas to you.
What cost did I incur?

'It is *a turkey* without doubt,'
Scrooge said with happy frown.
'You cannot carry that huge bird
Across to Camden Town.

'No – you must have a cab,' and so
It was all quickly done.
Scrooge chuckled as he paid for it.
He'd never had such fun.

He paid the boy and poulterer
Without the slightest care,
Then with another chuckle he
Sank breathless in his chair.

He chuckled till he nearly cried
And then with heaving chest,
He had a shave and dressed himself
All in his Sunday best.

People now were out about
Just as he'd seen before,
With Christmas Present's Spirit –
People by the score.

Scrooge walked along, hands tucked behind,
A smile upon his face;
He looked a pleasant fellow
Which was now quite the case.

So people said 'Good morning sir.'
A 'Merry Christmas' too.
And Scrooge with happy heart replied,
'Kind sir, the same to you.'

And often ever afterwards,
Scrooge said, in all the years
It was the sweetest sound he'd heard;
The blithest to his ears.

SCROOGE MAKES AMENDS

He'd not gone far when he espied
Appearing from a door,
One of the gentlemen who'd asked
For money for the poor.

The one who'd said so pleasantly,
'*Scrooge and Marley's*, sir?'
Scrooge felt a pang across his heart
For he had played the cur.

He dreaded how this gentleman
Would view him when they met,
But now his path led straight to him
As if it had been set.

And so he took it – headed on,
Quickening his pace.
He grasped the gentleman's two hands
And looked him in the face.

'My dear, dear sir. How do you do?
I do hope yesterday
You were successful and good sir
I'd also like to say…'

'Mr. Scrooge,' the man replied.
'That is my name I fear.
May I say Merry Christmas
And happiness next year.

'I know my name will likely be
Unpleasant to you so
I ask your pardon and I'd like
For you to also know…'

And here Scrooge whispered in his ear;
The gentleman then said,
'Lord bless me. Are you serious?'
Scrooge just inclined his head.

'If you please, I do insist.
And not a farthing less.
Back payments are included –
Please sir – don't make me press.

'I'd take it as a favour.'
The gentleman then said,
'I don't know what to say dear sir.'
Scrooge turned just slightly red.

'Please do not say a single word,'
Came Scrooge's fervent plea.
'Don't say a thing, but promise sir
You'll come to visit me.'

'I will, I will,' came his reply.
'Be sure it's what I'll do.'
Scrooge said, 'I thank you fifty times.
I'm much obliged to you.'

SCROOGE VISITS HIS CLOSEST KIN

Scrooge walked along the city streets
And watched the people go
About their business happily
As they rushed to and fro.

He patted children on the head
And had a little talk.
He never dreamt he'd have such fun
From just a simple walk.

Finally – that afternoon
He turned his steps unto
His nephews house, although not sure
What it was best to do.

He passed the door a dozen times,
Nervous and in shock.
He didn't have the courage
To go to it and knock.

But then at last he made a dash
To overcome his fear.
A young maid answered – Scrooge then asked,
'Is Fred at home, my dear?'

She replied, 'Yes sir,' and said,
'Because it's Christmas Day –
He's in the dining room upstairs.
I'll show you, sir, the way.'

'Thank'ee,' Scrooge replied, 'But I
Know quite well where to go
And it will be a great surprise,
Because he doesn't know…

'That I had planned to come today –
He will not mind I'm sure.'
So up the stairs he made his way
And opened up the door.

His relatives were in the room.
Scrooge quietly said, 'Fred.'
His niece by marriage started.
'Why bless my soul,' Fred said.

'What's this?' he carried on, surprised.
The shock was really huge.
Scrooge hesitated then replied,
''Tis I – your Uncle Scrooge.

'I've come for dinner Fred, will you
Allow me to come in?'
Let him in – for mercy's sake –
They were his closest kin.

Fred nearly shook his arm right off.
He said, 'With all my heart.'
And they embraced and there and then
They made another start.

And soon the other guests arrived,
And oh what fun they had,
A party truly wonderful
And everyone was glad,

That Uncle Scrooge was there – Fred said
In his so kindly way,
That he was overjoyed that Scrooge
Had come for Christmas Day.

THE END OF IT

Scrooge reached his office early –
Next morning he was there
Right on the very stroke of nine –
Oh he took special care…

To make quite sure that he'd arrive
To catch Bob coming late.
He wished to see Bob Cratchit
Get into a state.

And so he watched – the clock struck nine,
No sign of Bob at all.
Scrooge sat there waiting at his desk
To see what would befall.

And Bob was absent when the clock
Had struck the quarter past.
Then finally poor, flustered Bob
Came rushing in at last.

His hat was off before he reached
The Counting House front door;
Then to his desk and writing hard
In seconds – nothing more.

'Hallo!' growled Scrooge – he tried to sound
His normal rough, gruff way.
'What do you mean by coming here
At this late time of day?'

'I'm very sorry,' Bob replied.
'It's but a little crime.
I know I'm in the wrong and that
I am behind my time.'

'You are,' Scrooge said. 'Now step this way.'
Bob pleaded in his fear,
'It shall not be repeated sir.
It's only once a year.'

'Now listen carefully my friend,'
Scrooge's voice grew stronger.
'I will not stand for all of this,
Not for a moment longer.

'And therefore Bob,' cried happy Scrooge,
'Take heed to what I say.
For from this very moment on
I shall increase your pay.

'So Merry Christmas Bob,' Scrooge cried,
'And from now on you'll find
That I have changed.' – but scared Bob thought
Old Scrooge had lost his mind.

He wondered should he hold him down
And call for outside aid,
But when he saw Scrooge meant it
These thoughts began to fade.

'A merrier Christmas Bob,' Scrooge said –
His tone was now quite mellow –
'Than I have given you for years,
My honest, decent fellow.

'I'll raise your salary as I've said,
And help your children too.
We'll have a chat about affairs
And see what we can do.

'We'll make a plan and do it all
This very afternoon,
O'er a bowl of Christmas punch.'
Bob saw he'd changed his tune.

And then he wondered if it might
Be merely subterfuge,
But still he felt quite overjoyed
With this reformed, new Scrooge.

And Scrooge was better than his word.
He did so much and more
To bring some happiness and cheer
To poor Bob Cratchit's door.

For when he'd said he'd help them all
This hadn't been a lie,
And he did much for Tiny Tim
Which meant Tim didn't die.

And Scrooge became as good a man
As that old city knew,
Or any other city,
Or town or borough too.

Some people laughed to see him change,
But let them laugh he'd say;
It didn't matter if they laughed,
For this was just their way.

And his own heart laughed loudest there,
This was his choice and whim,
And he would smile and tell himself
'Twas good enough for him.

He had no further truck with Ghosts
And folk would often tell,
Scrooge was the man for Christmas
If you would keep it well.

For he could make it happy,
He knew how to contrive
To make it full of wonderment
Vibrant and alive.

And may this sentiment be true
For all of us – so we
Bring happiness, like Fezziwig,
To everyone we see;

And celebrate this special time –
Bring merriment and joy,
Especially to the children,
To every girl and boy,

And make the festive Christmas time
A season of such fun,
And join with Tiny Tim and say,
'God bless Us. Every One!'

Also by Richard Cuddington

SHAKESPEARE'S TRAGEDIES
IN EASY READING VERSE

Richard Cuddington applies his Easy Reading Verse to
Shakespeare's Tragedies. These are some of the Bard's
most famous and compelling plays. Retold here in simple
and engaging verse, the drama and excitement unfold with
an urgency and momentum that captures the essence of
the original plays.

Here the reader will meet Hamlet avenging his father's
murder, Romeo risking all for his Juliet, Othello borne
down with jealousy, Macbeth plotting to obtain Scotland's
crown and many other colourful and doomed characters.

The sheer drama of some of Shakespeare's most
memorable and highly acclaimed plays is captured here in
fast moving, entertaining verse.

And when you know what each play is about you may well
be encouraged to find out more about what makes these
people tick by venturing into the original texts, having
crept under the literary barrier and already found a way in
by the back door.

SHAKESPEARE'S COMEDIES IN EASY READING VERSE

Richard Cuddington offers his readers a new approach to Shakespeare which acknowledges the Bard's stature as England's finest poet and playwright but lays aside the trappings of that greatness to reveal what made him popular with his contemporary audiences and what can still enchant us today – the stories.

Here in Easy Reading Verse the author retells the stories of Shakespeare's Comedies with clarity, humour and a modern directness. Readers will meet Shylock demanding his pound of flesh, Jack Falstaff pursuing his 'merry wives', Petruchio taming his Katherine and many other unforgettable characters who leap off the page with the immediacy of cartoon personalities.

The straightforward language with its bouncing, infectious rhythms and uncomplicated verse add pace and humour to each story as it rapidly unfolds. In this way the author makes Shakespeare less intimidating to potential readers, showing that England's greatest playwright can be fun and encouraging all who enjoy these verses to sample the rich pleasure of the original work.

SHAKESPEARE'S HISTORIES & ROMANCES IN EASY READING VERSE

Here in Richard Cuddington's Easy Reading Verse are Shakespeare's Histories and Romances which take the reader on two separate journeys. One through various turbulent periods of English history – the other through the slightly calmer waters of romance.

All the stories are told in clear and rhythmic verse which enhances the many dramatic and romantic situations. Readers will be entranced by the very diversity and richness of the colourful plots.

Here we meet Richard the Second losing his throne, Henry the Fifth conquering the French at Agincourt and Richard the Third using all his dastardly wiles to keep the crown. In contrast the Romances will introduce Prospero whipping up a tempest, Pericles losing, then finding his Thaisa and Palamon and Arcite fighting for the hand of Emilia. A veritable pageant of drama, turmoil and intrigue is encapsulated in these enthralling stories which are truly some of the Bard's finest plays.

These adaptations are an enjoyable and riveting read and act as an excellent bridge to the original texts.

SHAKESPEARE'S SONNETS
IN EASY READING VERSE

Richard Cuddington's light-hearted adaptation of Shakespeare's Sonnets captures the essence of the original texts but in a way that makes them instantly accessible and understandable to the modern reader.

Originally published in 1609, many critics believe the Sonnets come closer to revealing Shakespeare the man, than any of his other works. Written in the first person, the Sonnets expose an emotional range that has given them enduring appeal.

The author now applies his straightforward Easy Reading Verse to create a fresh interpretation of the Sonnets. Here in simple and enjoyable lyrics, the mysteries of the Sonnets are unravelled, and with the original texts also contained within the book, they act as an aid in the understanding of Shakespeare's masterpieces.

CHAUCER'S CANTERBURY TALES
IN EASY READING VERSE

For all its great reputation and the affection in which it is
held, Chaucer's Canterbury Tales, written in 14th century
Middle English, can actually be a daunting prospect to read.
Richard Cuddington now steps in with a novel approach
to Chaucer's famous gallery of pilgrims with their tales of
chivalry, romance, courtly love, treachery, avarice,
bawdiness, humour and nobility.
Whether you're new to the tales, or perhaps a teacher
looking to enthuse and stimulate your students, or simply
thinking of re-reading them, you will find here a
thoroughly entertaining and immediately accessible way in
to the storytelling genius of Chaucer in simple and
amusing rhyming verse.

CHARLES DICKENS' OLIVER TWIST
IN EASY READING VERSE

Oliver Twist has been a family favourite ever since
Charles Dickens gave birth to his marvellous story in
1837. It has been reproduced in many ways but now
Richard Cuddington applies his Easy Reading Verse to
recount this famous tale.

Here are all the familiar cast of characters – brought to life
in fun, uplifting narrative verse that moves along at a
vibrant pace. From the moment of Oliver's birth in the
Workhouse, through all his adventures at the hands of
Fagin and Bill Sikes until he finally finds a new life – there
is never a dull moment.

The author has previously applied his straightforward,
rhythmic style to The Complete Works of Shakespeare
and Chaucer's Canterbury Tales and now turns to
Dickens' famous story to retell it in a way that will have
great appeal to children and adults alike.

KENNETH GRAHAME'S
THE WIND IN THE WILLOWS
IN EASY READING VERSE

Here is a delightful re-telling of one of Britain's best-loved books, aimed at younger children but also providing a treat for Grahame's established legion of fans of all ages. Richard Cuddington's verse rendition of Kenneth Grahame's The Wind in the Willows is the perfect introduction to a volume of stories which have enchanted generations of readers with its timeless evocation of life 'along the river bank'. All the well-known characters are here: the Mole, the Water Rat, Badger, Otter and, of course, the larger-than-life and utterly irrepressible Mr Toad of Toad Hall. The author has retained all the verve and energy of the original tales, but simplified the language to make them more accessible to the younger reader. Mole's frightening visit to the Wild Wood in the depths of winter and the colourful adventures of Toad take centre stage in bubbling rhythmic verse that drives the ebullient narrative forward so that there is never a dull moment.

www.ingramcontent.com/pod-product-compliance
Lightning Source LLC
Chambersburg PA
CBHW071825190726
48292CB00005B/1609